Critical Acclaim for PATRICIA MacLACHLAN's Novels

ARTHUR, FOR THE VERY FIRST TIME

"MacLachlan has created a wonderfully original and lovable group of people. The story has a deep tenderness, a gentle humor, and a beautifully honed writing style." —*The Bulletin of the Center for Children's Books*

An ALA Notable Book

CASSIE BINEGAR

"The writing is luminous; romantic ten- and twelve-year-old girls will love it all." —*School Library Journal*

THE FACTS AND FICTIONS OF MINNA PRATT

"A wonderfully wise and funny story that will be read and reread and relished for a long time." —*The Horn Book*

An ALA Notable Book

SARAH, PLAIN AND TALL

"A near-perfect miniature novel." —ALA *Booklist*

Newbery Medal Winner
An ALA Notable Book
Christopher Medal Winner
Scott O'Dell Award for Historical Fiction

SEVEN KISSES IN A ROW

"[A] brief understated story full of humor and the warmth of family caring and mutual affection." —*The Horn Book*

UNCLAIMED TREASURES

"A tender and subtle book that has strong characters, a flowing style, and a perceptive depiction of familial problems and loyalties."

—*The Bulletin of the Center for Children's Books*

A <u>Boston Globe</u>–<u>Horn Book</u> Award Honor Book
An ALA Notable Book

Also by
PATRICIA MacLACHLAN

§§

Through Grandpa's Eyes

Arthur, For the Very First Time

Mama One, Mama Two

Cassie Binegar

Unclaimed Treasures

The Facts and Fictions of Minna Pratt

Sarah, Plain and Tall

Skylark

Caleb's Story

Three Names

All the Places to Love

Seven Kisses in a Row

PATRICIA MacLACHLAN

Pictures by Maria Pia Marrella

A Charlotte Zolotow Book

HARPERTROPHY®

AN IMPRINT OF HARPERCOLLINS *PUBLISHERS*

Harper Trophy® is a registered trademark of
HarperCollins Publishers Inc.

Seven Kisses in a Row
Text copyright © 1983 by Patricia MacLachlan
Illustrations copyright © 1983 by Maria Pia Marrella
For information address HarperCollins Children's Books,
a division of HarperCollins Publishers,
1350 Avenue of the Americas, New York, NY 10019.

Library of Congress Cataloging-in-Publication Data
MacLachlan, Patricia.
    Seven kisses in a row.
        p.   cm.
    "A Charlotte Zolotow book."
    Summary: Emma learns to accept "different strokes for different
folks" when her aunt and uncle come to take care of her and her
brother.
    ISBN 0-06-024084-9 (lib. bdg.) — ISBN 0-06-440231-2 (pbk.)
    [1. Aunts—Fiction.   2. Uncles—Fiction.   3. Family life—
Fiction.]   I. Marrella, Maria Pia, ill.   II. Title.
PZ7.M2225Se   1983   82-47718
[Fic]   CIP
                                                              AC

First Harper Trophy edition, 1988

Visit us on the World Wide Web!
www.harperchildrens.com

This is Emily's book.

Contents

§ §

Seven Kisses in a Row

The morning sun came through the window curtains and made lace designs on Emma's bed. She got up and went to her parents' bedroom.

"It's morning," she called through the door. "It's time for divided grapefruit with a cherry in the middle."

There was no answer.

Emma opened the door and looked in. She had forgotten. Her mother and father were away for five days. Her father was an eyeball doctor, though he called it something else. He and her mother had gone to an eyeball meeting. Her aunt and uncle were sleeping in her parents' bed. Uncle Elliot with his face in the pillow and Aunt Evelyn with her mouth open.

Emma walked over to the bed and stood there. It wasn't fair, Emma thought, for her parents to go away and leave her with an aunt and uncle she hardly knew. Maybe they didn't know any children. What if they didn't *like* children? They probably didn't know anything at all about night lights and bad dreams and telling two whole stories before bedtime and no eggplant cooked in tomatoes. Emma leaned over to examine Uncle Elliot. He looked just like her father except that his hair wasn't disappearing like her father's. He was making funny noises into his pillow.

"Plah, oosh, plah, oosh."

Emma went around the bed to study Aunt Evelyn. She had lots of curly hair and pierced ears: one earring in one ear and two in the other. Emma frowned. That wasn't even.

"It's time for breakfast," said Emma.

Aunt Evelyn closed her mouth and opened her eyes.

"Later," she said.

"I'm hungry now," said Emma.

Aunt Evelyn didn't answer. She was asleep.

Emma went over to Uncle Elliot.

"Good morning," she said cheerfully.

Uncle Elliot made one big *oosh*ing sound into his pillow.

"I'm hungry," said Emma.

"*I'm* tired," said Uncle Elliot.

Emma frowned again.

"Would you give me seven kisses in a row?"

she asked. "Papa always gives me seven kisses in a row in the morning."

Uncle Elliot said nothing. He was asleep.

"*Plah, oosh, plah, oosh.*"

Emma went to the kitchen for something to eat. The cereal boxes were empty. Her big brother, Zachary, had eaten breakfast. Emma made three peanut butter and toast sandwiches. The peanut butter melted on the toast and ran down her chin.

She knocked on Zachary's door. He had his earphones on.

"It's morning," said Emma. "Uncle Elliot is *oosh*ing and Aunt Evelyn's ears aren't even. They're asleep. And I want divided grapefruit with a cherry in the middle."

"I hate grapefruit," said Zachary. "I don't even like to touch it."

"May I come in?" asked Emma.

Zachary shook his head.

"I'm writing a note to my girl friend, Miranda," he said. "And listening to my Morris Fibley record. It's private. Come back later."

Emma went downstairs and whispered awhile to her dog, Wayne. He turned over so Emma could scratch his stomach, but soon he fell asleep and twitched his legs, chasing a dream. He was not good company.

Emma ate four more pieces of toast and two apples and wished she had a parrot. She had read that parrots could talk and laugh. And that's what Emma wanted to do. Talk and laugh. Since she didn't have a parrot, she decided to run away. Just so everyone would know, she wrote a note:

Dear Aunt Evelyn, Dear Uncle Elliot (and Zachary, too),

When you wake up I will not be here. You did not make me devided greatfruit with a cherry. You did not give me seven kisses in a row. Papa always gives me seven kisses in a row. You did not let me listen to your Moris Fibly record. He sings flat anyway.

Emma found an old letter written to her father so she would know how to end the note. She wrote:

> *Fond regards to the family,*
> *Emma*

Emma packed a paper bag with five apples and one pear, some writing paper so she could write letters, and a grape Popsicle. If she had had a parrot she would have taken him, too. She walked down the street, past a brown dog who was watching a crack in the sidewalk, past the grocery store, past the post office, until she came to Mrs. Groundwine's house. Emma always went to

Mrs. Groundwine's house when she ran away.

Mrs. Groundwine was in her yard hanging sheets on the clothesline. She waved at Emma.

"Where are you headed, Emmy?" she called. Mrs. Groundwine was the only person in the world who called Emma Emmy.

"Running away," called Emma.

"Nice day for it," said Mrs. Groundwine. "But you got a little drip from your bag there."

"It must be my Popsicle," said Emma.

"Come in for a bit," invited Mrs. Groundwine. "I've got some biscuits just out of the oven."

"You don't have any divided grapefruits, do you?" asked Emma.

"No," said Mrs. Groundwine, "but I've got an orange, and you can see Molly's new kittens."

"How many kittens?" asked Emma as they walked inside.

"Seven," said Mrs. Groundwine proudly.

Seven made Emma think about seven kisses in a row.

Mrs. Groundwine's house was full of cats. They sat on the counters, the tables, the chairs, and Mrs. Groundwine.

"Do the cats like parrots?" asked Emma.

"No," said Mrs. Groundwine.

"Then it is good I don't have a parrot," said Emma.

7

She ate a warm biscuit and told Mrs. Groundwine that nobody loved her.

"My parents are away and my aunt and uncle are only practicing being parents. But they are asleep. And Zachary is too busy."

"Ah," said Mrs. Groundwine, nodding her head. "That's like my cats. Rosie there hasn't spoken to me in weeks. Minna only comes when she feels like it. And Molly is much too busy with her kittens now to give me any time. Sometimes they are busy being cats."

Emma thought about her parents, who were busy being away, and Aunt Evelyn and Uncle Elliot, who were busy being sleepy. And Zachary, who was busy being busy. Emma ate one more biscuit. It was too late for her Popsicle.

There was a knock at the door. Outside, Zachary stood on the porch with Emma's note in his hand.

"You spelled divided wrong," he said. "And grapefruit and Morris Fibley."

Emma and Zachary said good-bye to Mrs. Groundwine and the cats, who did not speak to them. Zach took Emma's hand and they walked back up the street again, past the post office, past the grocery store, and past the brown dog, who was now watching a hole by the side of the crack in the sidewalk.

"You should have told me you were lonely," said Zachary.

"I wasn't sure," said Emma, who liked holding hands with Zachary. "Are Aunt Evelyn and Uncle Elliot up yet?"

"No," said Zachary. "Do you want to hear my Morris Fibley record?"

Emma shook her head.

"I'm sleepy," she said, yawning.

"Do you want me to make you divided grapefruit with a cherry in the middle?"

"No," said Emma. "You hate grapefruit, Zach. And you don't like to touch it."

"That's true," agreed Zachary. He followed Emma into her bedroom and watched her get back into bed.

"There's only kisses left, I guess." He leaned over and gave Emma seven kisses in a row.

Emma smiled. "That's seven from you, seven from Uncle Elliot, and seven from Aunt Evelyn when they wake up," she said. "How many is that, Zach?"

"Twenty-one," said Zachary. He thought a bit. Then he gave Emma one more kiss. He knew most times she liked things even.

Rules

Aunt Evelyn and Uncle Elliot came with lots of rules. Rules about eating: how much and what to. Rules about sleeping: what time and how to. They had rules about cleaning and messing up, playing and resting, how to dress and when to.

In the morning Aunt Evelyn and Uncle Elliot exercised. Emma and Zach's parents did not exercise. They ran about a lot, but they did not call it exercising.

"Exercising twice a day is one of my rules," explained Uncle Elliot. "Once in the morning, once at night." He wore a torn sweat shirt and matching torn pants as he ran in place in front of the television. He made the same kinds of *oosh*ing sounds that he made when he slept. Aunt Evelyn did not make *oosh*ing sounds. She made no sounds at all as she bent her legs and arms in odd ways. First Aunt Evelyn twisted herself into the shape of a swan. Then a large U. Then a pretzel.

"Do you like what you're doing?" asked Emma.

"I love it!" exclaimed Aunt Evelyn. "It makes me feel like a bird. Free. Soaring! You should try it."

Emma did try it. But it didn't make her feel much like a bird. It hurt.

"Does Uncle Elliot like to exercise, too?" asked Zachary.

"NO!" shouted Uncle Elliot, *oosh*ing in front of the morning news. "But it's one of my rules, exercising is."

"I'll run with you," said Zachary. "We could run around the block."

"The block! That's a good idea," said Uncle Elliot. "We'll take the dog, too. Dogs love to run."

"Not Wayne," said Emma. "Wayne only likes to sit. Or lie down."

"Nonsense," said Uncle Elliot. He snapped the leash on Wayne's collar. Wayne lay down. "Come, Wayne! Up, Wayne! Run, Wayne!" urged Uncle Elliot. He pulled while Zachary pushed Wayne from behind. When they left, Emma and Aunt Evelyn smiled at each other.

"What would you like to do now?" asked Aunt Evelyn. "Maybe you have homework to do."

11

"It's only Saturday morning," said Emma. "I always do my homework late Sunday night."

Aunt Evelyn frowned. "Late Sunday night? When I was your age we had a rule to get our homework done early."

"You have lots of rules," said Emma. "We only have three rules. That's enough."

"Only three?" asked Aunt Evelyn. "What are they?"

Emma leaned her chin in her hand. "Number one: Be kind. Number two: No kicking or biting. Number three: Any rule can be changed."

Aunt Evelyn smiled. "You're right. Maybe that is just about enough rules."

Aunt Evelyn took some knitting out of a large bag. The knitting was bright purple with shiny silver spangles on it. Emma thought it was very jazzy.

"What are you knitting?" she asked.

"Baby booties," said Aunt Evelyn. "For the baby."

"What baby?"

"Our baby, your Uncle Elliot's and mine," said Aunt Evelyn. "It's kind of a secret."

"Does Uncle Elliot know?" asked Emma.

"Yes," said Aunt Evelyn. "Uncle Elliot knows. And you, and your mother and father. That's about all."

Emma thought about the new baby. She pictured it looking like Aunt Evelyn, short curly black hair, three earrings, purple spangled booties. It would be, Emma knew, a very jazzy baby. And it would have lots and lots of rules. Emma watched as Aunt Evelyn took one finished spangled bootie out of her knitting bag. The bootie was extremely large, almost large enough for Emma. Emma looked at the silver spangles. She thought a moment.

"Aunt Evelyn, I'm very glad about your baby."

"Ditto," said Aunt Evelyn.

"What does ditto mean?" asked Emma.

"It means 'me too,'" said Aunt Evelyn.

"Aunt Evelyn," said Emma, "I have something bad to tell you."

"What's that?" asked Aunt Evelyn.

"Your baby will eat those spangles." Emma pointed to the baby booties.

"Oh dear," said Aunt Evelyn. "I suppose you are right. I don't know very much about babies."

Emma felt sorry for Aunt Evelyn.

"Don't worry, Aunt Evelyn, I was a baby about seven years ago. And my mother told me what I was like."

Aunt Evelyn put her arm around Emma. "You'd better tell me all about it," she said.

"First of all," Emma began, "babies don't pay attention to rules. They will eat spangles on booties, and wet and spit up milk and cry and wake up and sleep whenever they want to."

Aunt Evelyn sighed. "That's true, isn't it?"

Emma nodded. She looked at the purple spangled booties.

"Aunt Evelyn, I have something more bad to tell you."

"Now what?" asked Aunt Evelyn.

"Those purple booties are much too big for your baby," said Emma. "But I have some in my room that I saved from when I was a baby. They are not purple. I could give them to you."

Aunt Evelyn smiled at Emma. "Only if you want to, Emma."

Emma went into her room and found the booties. They were pink and blue. And they were very small. Aunt Evelyn loved them.

"Emma," she said, "I have noticed something. I think the purple spangled booties will fit you."

"I knew that," said Emma.

Aunt Evelyn laughed. "Oh, Emma. I like you."

"Ditto," said Emma.

After a while Uncle Elliot and Zachary came back from running. Zachary was carrying Wayne's leash. Uncle Elliot was carrying Wayne. He put

Wayne down and Wayne found his favorite sun spot on the floor and lay down. Uncle Elliot lay down on the couch.

"That was fun," said Zachary.

"No, it was not fun," said Uncle Elliot. "That dog wouldn't run."

"I know," said Emma. "Wayne has his own rules and they are not about exercising. They are about sitting, lying down, sleeping, and eating."

"Just like babies," said Aunt Evelyn.

"Could I exercise with you tonight, Uncle Elliot?" asked Zach.

Uncle Elliot moaned. "I don't know, Zach. I'm so tired that I may have to break my rule about exercising twice a day."

"That's all right, dear," said Aunt Evelyn. "Rules can be changed."

"Now *that's* a wonderful rule," said Uncle Elliot with lots of feeling.

"I think so, too," said Aunt Evelyn.

"Ditto," said Emma.

Broccoli

Emma set the table for dinner.

"We have no lowercase spoons," she said. "Only capitals."

"Capitals are fine," said Aunt Evelyn, smiling.

Zachary came to the table wearing his favorite false nose and glasses. Uncle Elliot came wearing his own nose and his own glasses. Emma came with dirty hands.

"Wash the backs of your hands, too," said Aunt Evelyn.

"But I don't eat with the backs," Emma protested.

"You don't eat off the backs of the plates, either," said Uncle Elliot. "But we wash them."

Emma washed her hands.

"What are we having for dinner?" asked Zachary.

"Lots of healthy things," said Aunt Evelyn happily.

Emma frowned. She saw meat loaf, potatoes, and salad, and something green in a bowl. It was not eggplant cooked in tomatoes. It was something else bad.

"What is that?" asked Emma.

"That is broccoli," said Uncle Elliot.

"May I have cold cereal?" asked Emma.

"No you may not," said Aunt Evelyn. She served dinner.

"Don't let the potatoes and gravy touch the salad!" cried Emma.

"It doesn't make any difference," said Zachary. "They all mix together in your stomach anyway."

"Don't talk about stomachs at the table," said Emma, squeezing up her face and fluttering her hand. She tipped over her glass of milk. It made a river across the table and into Zachary's lap. He jumped up.

"I can't eat here," he said. He took his plate and chair and sat in the corner facing the wall. Emma and Uncle Elliot cleaned up the table. Wayne lapped some of the milk up off the floor and lay down waiting for more.

"Now," said Uncle Elliot, "let's all eat up!"

"Where does broccoli come from?" asked Emma.

"It's a plant," said Aunt Evelyn. "Try some."

"I can't," said Emma.

"Of course you can," said Uncle Elliot. "I can eat anything. You can eat anything."

"You should have eaten it first," said Zachary to the wall. "Before it got tired out."

Emma touched her broccoli.

"It's too late," she said. "I can't eat it."

"And why not?" asked Uncle Elliot sternly.

"Because the broccoli is moving on my plate," said Emma.

Aunt Evelyn laughed. Zachary laughed. Uncle Elliot did not laugh.

"That's silly," he said. "Your broccoli is not alive. So it could not move."

"It was alive once," said Emma. "It grew somewhere—Aunt Evelyn said so. And it was alive."

"Well, it's not alive now, Emma," said Uncle Elliot. "So it can't move."

"Then I can't eat it now," said Emma.

"Why?" asked Uncle Elliot.

"Because it is dead," said Emma. "I cannot eat a dead broccoli."

Zachary laughed very loudly and for a long time.

"Zachary," said Aunt Evelyn, "you're not helping. And don't tip back in your chair."

"Why?" asked Zachary.

"Because you'll fall over backward and hurt yourself," said Aunt Evelyn.

"And you'll break the chair," added Uncle Elliot. He looked at Emma. "Broccoli is good for you," he said. "Don't you want to be healthy?"

"No," said Emma.

"Or have strong bones and shiny teeth?" asked Uncle Elliot.

"I can't see my bones," said Emma. "And I don't have to smile."

"That's funny," said Zachary.

Aunt Evelyn and Uncle Elliot looked at each other and sighed. They picked up their empty plates and went into the kitchen. Zachary sighed, too. He went over to Emma's chair.

"Don't you want cherry glimmer ice cream for dessert?" he asked.

Emma looked up, surprised. "Is that what Aunt Evelyn and Uncle Elliot are having for dessert?"

Zachary nodded. Emma and Zach's parents never bought cherry glimmer ice cream for dessert. Emma's father said it tasted as if it were made from unreal cherries. They always served fruit, or told Emma and Zach that they must be much too full for dessert.

"Yes," said Emma. "I want cherry glimmer ice cream for dessert."

"Then eat your broccoli," Zach said. "Be-

sides"—he leaned over to whisper in her ear—"everything moves if you look at it long enough."

Emma looked up at Zachary. Then she looked at her broccoli. "You're a good brother, Zach," she said.

Zachary was right. The broccoli moved off Emma's plate. She cut it up into twenty-two tiny pieces and swallowed them like vitamins just in case she wanted strong bones and shiny teeth.

The cherry glimmer ice cream moved off her plate even faster.

Love and Marriage
and Miranda

Aunt Evelyn looked out the window.

"There is a person with fuzzy hair coming up the walk," she announced.

"That's Miranda!" exclaimed Zachary. "My girl friend."

Emma followed Zachary to the front door.

"Why is she here?" asked Emma.

"She likes me," said Zachary.

"That doesn't mean she has to come to the house," said Emma.

Miranda's hair was even more fuzzy in the house, as if she had shaken hands with the light sockets. Emma saw that she had a ring on every single finger, and she was wearing high-heeled shoes that were too big for her.

Zachary introduced Miranda to Uncle Elliot and Aunt Evelyn. Uncle Elliot was reading the Sunday newspaper beginning with the first page right through to the last. In order. Emma didn't know anyone who read the Sunday paper that way. Emma's mother and father had peppy discussions over who would get which section first. Once Emma's mother hid the section she wanted under the couch.

Aunt Evelyn was knitting something very large and gray. Perhaps for a whale. Emma hoped it was for Uncle Elliot and not for the new baby.

"Hi, Emma," said Miranda.

"Are those your mother's shoes?" asked Emma.

"Yes," said Miranda. She sat down and crossed her legs, and one shoe fell off.

Emma peered at Miranda.

"Was your hair like that when you were born?" she asked.

"No," said Miranda. "I did it myself. I could do it to your hair, too, if you want."

"Never," said Emma.

"Would you like to listen to my Morris Fibley record?" Zachary asked Miranda.

"Sure," said Miranda. "I came over because I was bored. It's my mother and father's wedding anniversary and they've gone out to hold hands and eat steak with whipped potatoes by candle-light."

"In the middle of the day?" asked Emma.

Miranda shrugged her shoulders. "It's romantic, they said. It goes with love and marriage. Also they couldn't get a sitter for me tonight."

Emma knew Miranda's parents. Miranda's mother was very short, nearly a midget, and she wore wigs. Miranda's father smiled all the time, even if there was nothing to smile about. Maybe his wife's wigs made him happy.

Zachary and Miranda went off to listen to his Morris Fibley record, and Emma sat down on the arm of Aunt Evelyn's chair and thought about love and marriage and Miranda. She wondered if Zachary would marry fuzzy Miranda and have lots of children whose hair stood up. They could, she supposed, wear hats, or wigs like Miranda's mother. Miranda and Zachary were listening to the music, probably holding hands by now, getting closer to love and marriage.

It was quiet in the living room. The only sounds were the clicking of Aunt Evelyn's knitting needles and the rustle of Uncle Elliot's newspaper. Emma got tired of worrying quietly.

"He'll probably show her all his bottle caps!" Emma said very loudly, making Uncle Elliot jump. "And his dirt collection. I'm the only one who's smelled every jar of his dirt collection. And he'll probably give her his Morris Fibley sweat shirt with the streak of lightning on it. The one he promised to give me when it's too small for him!"

"Don't you like Miranda?" asked Uncle Elliot, looking around his newspaper.

Emma thought a moment.

"Only by herself," she said.

"What does that mean?" asked Uncle Elliot.

Aunt Evelyn put down her whale knitting.

"It means," she said, "that Emma is a younger sister. Like me. I have two older brothers, Emma."

Uncle Elliot went back behind his newspaper.

"Did your brothers get married?" asked Emma.

"Yes," said Aunt Evelyn. "One even gave me his pet snake when he left."

"Do you still have it?" asked Emma, interested.

"No," said Uncle Elliot very softly behind the newspaper.

"Emma, they had lots of girl friends. I was jealous. Just the way they were jealous of some of my boyfriends. But they got married and we're still friends," said Aunt Evelyn. "Brothers and sisters are always brothers and sisters. And that has nothing to do with love and marriage. You'll see."

"Not me," said Emma, who couldn't think of one boy to love and marry and make Zachary jealous about. "I don't think I'll get married. I think I'd rather live by myself and raise seals in the bathtub."

"You may feel differently later," said Aunt Evelyn. "I did. I felt fluttery. Bubbly."

"Like heartburn?" asked Emma, making Uncle Elliot laugh.

"No," said Aunt Evelyn. "Romantic fluttery and bubbly. Uncle Elliot made me feel that way."

Emma moved over to the couch and looked at Uncle Elliot. He did not look romantic to her. He looked embarrassed.

"Do you know what your Uncle Elliot did before we got married?" asked Aunt Evelyn with a smile.

"Evelyn," said Uncle Elliot.

"What?" asked Emma. "What did he do?"

"He hired a skywriter to write I LOVE YOU EVELYN up in the sky. The pilot wrote I LOVE YOU EVEN by mistake. But it was romantic. It made me feel fluttery and bubbly."

"You did that?" Emma asked Uncle Elliot. She moved over closer to him and stared at him behind the newspaper.

"Then," Aunt Evelyn went on, "on our first anniversary . . ."

"Ev!" Uncle Elliot grinned and turned red.

"What?" asked Emma, smiling.

"He wrote a poem," said Aunt Evelyn, "and put it on a big sign in the front yard for everyone to see. I still remember it. To this very day. The poem was very romantic."

"What did it say?" asked Emma. She could hardly believe that her Uncle Elliot, who read the newspaper from the first page to the last in order, who cared mostly about exercising and rules, could also compose a romantic poem.

Aunt Evelyn cleared her throat and sat up straight. She recited:

> *"I love you Evelyn,*
> *I love you lots.*
> *When we're apart*
> *Life truly rots."*

There was a silence.

"That's beautiful," said Emma softly.

"You think so?" asked Uncle Elliot, pleased. "Do you *really* think so?"

"Yes," said Emma. "It is truly beautiful," she added, because Emma thought the word "truly" in Uncle Elliot's poem was the most beautiful thing of all.

Aunt Evelyn beamed. "Love and marriage," she said. "It all goes with love and marriage."

When Aunt Evelyn went into the kitchen, Emma stared at Uncle Elliot some more. She tugged at his sleeve.

"What are you going to give Aunt Evelyn for this year's anniversary?"

Uncle Elliot thought.

"I might rent a balloon and go up, or take her down the rapids in a rubber raft. Or maybe have the poem she likes engraved on a silver bracelet." He looked at Emma. "Gold's expensive."

Emma nodded.

"I think the balloon ride could make the baby dizzy," she said. "And riding down the rapids in a rubber raft might make Aunt Evelyn sick."

"Me, too," confessed Uncle Elliot.

"The bracelet is a good idea," said Emma. She thought how lucky Aunt Evelyn would be to have a bracelet with a large dangle on it with the romantic rotting poem engraved there. That was, Emma thought, almost as good as seals in the bathtub.

Miranda and Zachary were through listening to the record.

"I'd better go home now and see if my parents' wedding anniversary is over," said Miranda. "Every year my mother gets a new wig and a stainless steel pot."

"My mother got a pair of soft lenses this year," said Zachary, whose father, after all, was an eye-ball doctor.

Emma watched Miranda put on her jacket and wiggle all her rings around so that the stones sat on top. She wondered if it was healthy to wear so many rings. She watched as Miranda bent over to adjust her shoe straps so that her mother's shoes would stay on.

"Miranda," said Emma, "are you feeling fluttery and bubbly?"

"Why?" Miranda straightened up and looked alarmed. "Is there something going around?" She stuck out her tongue and looked in the hall mirror.

"Do *you* feel fluttery and bubbly, Zach?" asked Emma.

"No," said Zachary. "Is there something catching?"

"I guess," said Emma, smiling at the two of them, "that what is catching is not here yet."

Night Rumbles

"I am not going to sleep in my bedroom tonight," announced Emma.

"Why not?" asked Zachary. "Because of the mess?"

"No," said Emma. "Because of night rumbles."

"What are night rumbles?" asked Zachary.

"I am not sure," said Emma, "but my friend Noah has them. He says they only come at night. He says they will come here soon. They are furry things with legs who live in the closet, and whiskery shadows in the corners of the room, and a long arm that lives under the bed and tries to grab you when you jump into bed."

"Have you seen them yet?" asked Zachary.

Emma shook her head. "Not yet. And I am not going to."

"Where will you sleep?" asked Zachary.

"In the backyard," said Emma. "In the tent."

"In the tent!" exclaimed Zachary. He loved sleeping in the tent. "But what about bugs and grubs and wild wolves?"

"I am not afraid of bugs and grubs," said Emma. "And Wayne will protect me from wild wolves. In the tent there are not a lot of corners with boxes and closets and chairs and toy chests for things to hide in. Or in back of. Or under."

"No mess," said Zachary, nodding.

"No mess," agreed Emma. She began to pack her things.

Uncle Elliot poked his head in the door.

"Where are you going?"

"Emma is not going to sleep in her room tonight," said Zachary. "Because of night rumbles. The furry things with legs who live in the closet, and the whiskery shadows in the corners of the room, and the long arm that lives under the bed and tries to grab you when you jump into bed."

"Where?" asked Uncle Elliot, peering cautiously around the room.

"They only come at night," said Emma. "When the lights are off."

"You could leave the lights on," suggested Uncle Elliot.

Emma shook her head. "Then I'd see them," she said. She looked at Uncle Elliot. "My parents say there are no such things as night rumbles."

33

"And I am sure they are right," said Uncle Elliot heartily. He opened the closet door. "No furry things here," he said.

"They're hiding behind the shoe boxes," said Emma.

Uncle Elliot looked in each corner of Emma's room.

"There are no whiskery shadows," he said.

"They're waiting for you to leave," said Emma.

Uncle Elliot got down and peered under the bed.

"No arm," he announced.

"There will be," said Emma. "I am going to sleep outside in the tent."

"The tent! All by yourself?" exclaimed Uncle Elliot. "Won't you be scared? I was always scared."

"I could sleep out there with you," said Zachary eagerly.

"No," said Emma. "By myself. I'll have Wayne. And my battery lamp and my pencils and pens and writing paper and some books and two doughnuts that I've saved for a long time and Eleanor, my cactus."

"Just remember bugs and grubs and wild wolves," whispered Zachary.

They went to the garage to look for the tent. Aunt Evelyn was doing her ballet exercises with her hand on the car door handle.

"We're putting up the tent, Ev," said Uncle Elliot. "Emma's going to sleep outside tonight because of the night rumbles."

Aunt Evelyn looked at Emma. She raised her eyebrows.

Emma sighed. "The furry things with legs who live in the closet," she explained again, "and the whiskery shadows in the corners of the room, and the long arm that lives under the bed and tries to grab you when you jump into bed. My mother and father and Uncle Elliot do not think there are such things."

"Great loving George!" exclaimed Aunt Evelyn. "Of course there are! I slept in my closet for two weeks because of the *Whispers*."

"The *Whispers*?" Emma moved closer to Zachary.

"The *Whispers* rustled and murmured all night long in my room when I was your age," said Aunt Evelyn. "But won't you be lonely out in the tent by yourself? I would be real lonely."

"No," said Emma. "I'll have Wayne."

"I'd be lonely," said Aunt Evelyn.

Zachary and Uncle Elliot carried the tent out to the backyard.

"Can we put it up on the little hill?" asked Emma.

Zachary shook his head. "Everything will fall out the front door of the tent. You will, too."

"How about under the tree?" suggested Emma.

"The acorns will fall on the tent roof," said Zachary.

"That will not be good," said Emma. "Wayne barks at dropping acorns."

Finally they decided on a flat place in the middle of the yard where it would be easy for Wayne to watch for wild wolves.

Zachary helped Uncle Elliot put up the tent. He helped when Uncle Elliot tried to put up the tent upside down. He helped pound in the tent stakes when Uncle Elliot put them in the wrong place. He straightened the ropes so that the tent would not lean to one side. He helped by getting a bandage and ice when Uncle Elliot hit his finger with a hammer.

"It's done," called Uncle Elliot, collapsing on the ground and crawling inside the tent to pant in the shade.

Later, Emma moved all her things to the tent. Zachary did not help. She moved her sleeping bag first, and her Martha Mouse pillow. She moved her battery lamp and her pencils and pens and paper and books and old doughnuts and Eleanor, her cactus. Then Emma waited for nighttime. She ate dinner early so that she could get into the tent before the night rumbles came to her room. Zachary took a twenty-seven-minute shower and left soggy towels and cold puddles on the floor. Emma took a bubblebath and lost a herd of plastic animals and three marbles under the suds. Then it was nighttime.

"Good night Emma," said Uncle Elliot. "Are you sure you won't be scared?"

"No," said Emma. "I won't be scared."

"Will you be lonely?" asked Aunt Evelyn.

"No."

"Don't you want me to come too?" asked Zachary.

"No," said Emma. "Come, Wayne."

"Remember bugs and grubs and wild wolves," called Zachary as Emma padded out to the tent.

It was quiet and peaceful in the tent, and Wayne fell asleep right away, snorting and wheezing a bit. Emma read a chapter of her book, ate half an old doughnut, then watched the stars outside the tent flap. She closed her eyes.

"Emma." She woke up with a start as Zachary climbed inside the tent, dragging his sleeping bag. "Were you asleep already?"

"Yes," said Emma.

"I'm sorry I scared you about bugs and grubs and wild wolves," said Zachary. "I wanted to sleep in the tent with you."

"That's all right," said Emma. "You can stay for a while."

Emma moved over, and together they rolled Wayne farther into the corner.

"Good night, Emma."

"Good night, Zach."

It was quiet and peaceful again and Zachary fell asleep right away.

"Emma?" Just as Emma was about to fall asleep, she saw Aunt Evelyn crouched down with a thermos in her hand. "I thought you must be lonely. And thirsty. I brought you some hot chocolate."

Emma smiled. "Zach's here. Come in."

Aunt Evelyn crawled inside the tent. She lay down next to Emma. She yawned. "Now you won't be lonely," she said.

Emma drank some hot chocolate and watched Aunt Evelyn fall asleep. She wiggled back inside her sleeping bag, gently moving Wayne's head with her foot, and waited for Uncle Elliot.

"*Psst.* Emma."

"Yes, Uncle Elliot."

"Are you scared? Hey, everyone's here." He crawled over Zachary and pushed Wayne's rump around. "Got any doughnuts left?"

Together they watched the stars while Uncle Elliot ate a doughnut. He lay down next to

Zachary. "Boy," he said just before he fell asleep, "this isn't scary at all, is it?"

Emma turned over carefully and counted the stars. She thought about the bugs and grubs sleeping deep underneath the tent. She watched awhile for wild wolves. But she didn't worry. There was no room for wild wolves in the tent. Emma smiled and closed her eyes. No room for the *Whispers*, whoever they were. And no room at all for night rumbles.

Different Strokes

Aunt Evelyn squeezed between Emma's bedroom door and some boxes. She stepped over a pile of clothes, picked up two plates and three stuffed animals, jumped over a chair, and sat on Emma's bed. She looked around.

"You know, I think there is something here we need to do before your parents come home day after tomorrow."

"Do you mean pierce my ears?" asked Emma.

"I was thinking about your room," said Aunt Evelyn. "We could surprise your parents."

"My parents are never surprised," said Emma.

"Well, this room needs something," said Aunt Evelyn.

Emma looked around.

"We could paint the walls lavender," she said.

"Wrong," said Aunt Evelyn.

Emma grinned. "I know you mean cleaning

it," she said. "But I'd still rather have my ears pierced."

"You could start by clearing a walking path," suggested Aunt Evelyn.

"I like everything out in the open this way," said Emma. "I can see where everything is."

Aunt Evelyn opened Emma's bureau drawers. Emma's clothes popped up and peeked out.

"There are too many clothes in these drawers," said Aunt Evelyn. "You should get rid of all the things you don't wear."

"I like them all," protested Emma. "Even the things that are too small."

"I roll everything into little sausage rolls," said Uncle Elliot, who was standing in the doorway. "Then everything fits."

"That's because Uncle Elliot is a saver," said Aunt Evelyn. "He has so many things he has to roll them into sausage rolls."

"Different strokes," said Uncle Elliot, shrugging his shoulders.

"What does different strokes mean?" asked Emma.

"Different people do things in different ways," said Uncle Elliot. "They like different things. Different strokes for different folks."

Emma looked around.

"I like that," she said. "This is my stroke."

"Not while I'm in charge," said Aunt Evelyn. "Clean up. Find places for all those stuffed animals. There are too many for this room."

"Too many!" exclaimed Emma. "I need them all. They all have names."

"Even that one?" asked Aunt Evelyn, pointing.

"That's J.R., for Just Rabbit," said Emma. "He's my favorite."

"He only has one ear," said Uncle Elliot.

"That's all he needs for hearing," said Emma. "Different strokes."

"Maybe Zachary can help you," said Aunt Evelyn. "His room is always neat. He even has empty drawers."

Aunt Evelyn went into Zachary's room. Her feet made crunching noises on the floor.

"Why, Zach," she exclaimed, "what is all of this? Your room is always so neat and clean."

"It is neat and clean underneath all of this stuff," said Zachary. "I am cleaning out my collections."

"What am I stepping on?" asked Aunt Evelyn.

"His bottle caps," said Emma. "He has one thousand and two."

"You're standing on two," said Zachary.

"I always wanted to save bottle caps," said Uncle Elliot wistfully.

"And what's that?" asked Aunt Evelyn.

43

"That is my dirt collection," said Zachary. "It is all labeled. This jar is from Miranda's garden. This is from the baseball field. This is from the swamp."

"Ugh," said Aunt Evelyn. "That one smells terrible."

"I had a collection of door knockers once," said Uncle Elliot. "My mother made me give it away. It took up too much room. Bottle caps don't take up much room."

"I never heard of a door knocker collection before," said Zachary. "That's interesting."

Uncle Elliot looked at Aunt Evelyn. "Different strokes," he said.

When Aunt Evelyn left, Uncle Elliot and Zachary went into Emma's room. Emma's clothes had slithered out of her drawers and were hanging down onto the floor.

"What can I do?" asked Emma.

"Folding would be a good thing," said Zachary. "My clothes are folded. That is why I have empty drawers."

Zachary showed Emma how to fold very neatly. He folded her shirts in three parts and her pants in two parts, and he rolled her socks together like snowballs.

"Everything fits!" said Emma happily. "But what about my stuffed animals?"

"Hmm," said Uncle Elliot. He thought. "How about hibernation?"

"Hibernation where?" asked Emma.

"Hibernation in Zachary's empty drawers," said Uncle Elliot.

Emma smiled. "That's a good idea."

Zachary thought it was a good idea, too, and they sorted the stuffed animals. There were seventy-three counting J.R., who was missing an ear. They carried twenty into Zachary's room and carefully put them into his two empty drawers.

"Uncle Elliot was a big help," said Emma.

"We should do something nice for him," said Zachary.

Emma thought. She thought about her stuffed animals. She could give him one, but they all had names.

"I could give him my Morris Fibley sweat shirt," said Zachary. "But it's too small." Zachary smiled. "There is one thing I know Uncle Elliot likes."

"What?" asked Emma.

Zachary held up his bag of bottle caps.

"Uncle Elliot always wanted a bottle cap collection," he said. "But I did promise to give it to you when I didn't need it anymore."

"That's all right, Zach," said Emma. "There is still your dirt collection. I have always loved

your bottle caps. But I think Uncle Elliot loves them even more."

Uncle Elliot did love the bottle cap collection. He put it in one of the drawers under his sausage roll clothes.

"This will be our secret," he told Emma and Zach. "I'll surprise Evelyn when we get home."

Later, Aunt Evelyn came into Emma's room to check.

"Wonderful!" she exclaimed. "You even got rid of some of your old stuffed animals."

"There are twenty stuffed animals not in this room," said Emma truthfully.

"And I gave my bottle cap collection away," said Zachary.

"That's nice, Zachary," said Aunt Evelyn. "It will make someone very happy."

"Yes, it will," said Zachary.

"Now that you've cleaned up, I will do something about your ears, Emma," said Aunt Evelyn.

"You mean pierce them!" said Emma, delighted.

"Not quite," said Aunt Evelyn. She took out a pen and drew small flowers right in the middle of Emma's earlobes. The flowers looked just like earrings.

Emma looked in the mirror. "They're beautiful, Aunt Evelyn."

"I think they look a little dumb," said Zachary, peering over her shoulder.

"Different strokes, Zach," said Emma, looking at one ear, then the other. "Different strokes."

Lessons

There was a knock at Emma's door.

"Emma? Are you awake?" called Uncle Elliot.

There was no answer.

"It's morning," said Uncle Elliot through the door. "Time for divided grapefruit with a cherry in the middle. And seven kisses."

"I'm asleep," called Emma. "Come back later."

"She is not asleep," said Zachary out in the hall.

Uncle Elliot opened the door. There was a big lump that was Emma in the middle of the bed.

"What's the matter, Emma?"

"How did you know I was awake?" asked Emma from under the blankets.

"I guessed," said Uncle Elliot. "Don't you want to get up? It's our last day here before your parents come home. We'll do something special."

Emma groaned. "I'm very sick," she said. "My

49

head is squishy, my ears are numb, my feet are prickly."

"Probably she is not sick," said Zachary.

Uncle Elliot sat down and reached under the blankets to feel Emma's head.

"You're not hot," he said.

"Hotness is not part of my sickness," said Emma. She poked her head out of the covers. "I did have spots. They are gone now."

"Spots! Where were those spots?" asked Uncle Elliot.

"She never has spots," whispered Zachary.

"On my feet and ears," said Emma, glaring at Zachary.

"That sounds like calling the doctor," said Uncle Elliot.

"No!" Emma sat up in bed. "The doctor does not like me. She has a cold heart-listener. She puts an ear looker in my ears and sticks that Popsicle stick down my throat. Also, she is on vacation."

"I'll bet the doctor is not on vacation," said Zachary.

"What's the trouble?" asked Aunt Evelyn.

"I'm catching," said Emma. "And probably you and Uncle Elliot and Zachary and Wayne are, too. You had better call my parents and tell them not to come home for a week or three months."

Aunt Evelyn thought for a moment. "Even if we asked them to, I don't think they would stay away, Emma."

Uncle Elliot nodded. "They have not told you so yet," he said, "but I am sure they've missed you."

"Yes," said Emma. "They always miss me when they go to an eyeball meeting. They bring me place mats and postcards of hotels and city parks."

"Papa brings me new dirt for my dirt collection," said Zachary. "And colored eyeball pictures. I use them for my dart board."

"So there you see," said Aunt Evelyn. "They love you and will want to come back even though you are very sick and catching."

"I know she is not sick and catching," announced Zachary.

"How about breakfast in bed?" said Uncle Elliot. "Divided grapefruit right here."

"Our parents don't allow us to have breakfast in bed," said Zachary. "Because of the crumbs."

"Crumbs don't come with grapefruit," said Emma, sitting up.

"We'll all have breakfast in bed," said Uncle Elliot.

There were oranges and grapefruit and cereal and toast. There were lots of crumbs, too. But only for a little while, because Wayne came and cleaned them all up.

"I'm sorry you're not feeling better," said Uncle Elliot. "Today you were going to give me more father lessons."

"Emma doesn't have to give you father lessons if she doesn't feel well," said Aunt Evelyn. "We'll go to classes once a week when we get home."

"Once a week is not enough to learn how to be a father," said Emma.

"I know a lot already," said Uncle Elliot. "You have taught me about divided grapefruit and seven kisses in a row."

"And how to wash and feed and diaper," added Emma.

"How to diaper?" Aunt Evelyn said, surprised. "When did you learn about diapering?"

"Yesterday," said Uncle Elliot. "We practiced on Emma's doll, Mavis. Emma put water on the diaper. It was very real."

"There is more," said Emma.

"More than washing and feeding and diapering and divided grapefruit and seven kisses?" asked Uncle Elliot.

Emma nodded. She went over to the closet and took out Mavis, who was bald with only one eye that worked. She wrapped Mavis in a blanket and handed her to Uncle Elliot.

"Lullabies," she said.

Uncle Elliot put Mavis up on his shoulder and rubbed her back. Aunt Evelyn smiled.

"Lullabies," said Emma, "so that the baby will not scream all night and have terrible dreams."

"I don't know any lullabies," said Uncle Elliot.

"Make one up," said Emma.

Uncle Elliot thought. "How about," he began,

"Baby, baby, stop your screams.
Go to sleep and dream sweet dreams."

Zachary and Aunt Evelyn laughed.

"That's good, Uncle Elliot," said Emma. "The baby will like that lullaby."

"So am I now a father?" asked Uncle Elliot. "Do I pass?"

"Just one more thing," said Emma.

"What is that?" asked Uncle Elliot, burping Mavis.

"Talking to the baby," said Emma. "Most mothers and fathers and aunts and uncles do not talk right to babies. They talk baby talk to them. And that makes babies bored. They cry a lot and fall off beds to get attention. Talk to Mavis."

"No baby talk?" asked Uncle Elliot.

Emma shook her head. "No itsies or do-dos," she warned.

"Not even a goo?"

"No goos," said Emma.

Uncle Elliot put Mavis on his knee and held both her arms. Her one eye rolled up and looked at him.

"Welcome, Mavis, old shoe," he said. "You're not a half bad baby, actually. You only cry at night when I'm trying to sleep, you only spit up on my clean shirts, and you're only wet most of the time. You only rolled off the bed once. You eat everything but strained broccoli."

Emma and Zachary laughed.

"Pretty soon," said Uncle Elliot, "you will get to know your cousins, Emma and Zachary. You will learn all about bottle cap collections and night rumbles and strange spots that come and go. You will see them soon, because in my pocket I have two bus tickets for them to keep until you are born and they can come for a visit all by themselves to watch you burp and spit up. What do you say, old bald Mavis, do you think they will like that? And do you think I have passed yet?"

There was a silence. Uncle Elliot gave Mavis to Aunt Evelyn and took the two tickets out of his pocket. He handed one to Emma and one to Zachary.

Emma grinned at him.

"You know a whole lot about being a father, Uncle Elliot," said Emma.

"And a whole lot about being an uncle," added Zachary.

"He does now," said Aunt Evelyn, patting bald Mavis. "But he didn't before we knew you. We hardly knew any children before we knew you."

"I know," said Emma. She looked up at Uncle Elliot. "You passed, Uncle Elliot."

Uncle Elliot put one arm around Emma and one around Zachary.

"You did too," he said.

LULLABY

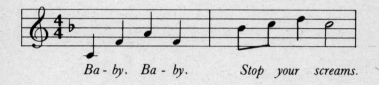

Ba - by, Ba - by.   Stop your screams.

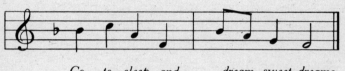

Go   to sleep and   dream sweet dreams.